Fairy Tale
Twists

For my wonderful Mum.
Thank you for everything x
K.D.

For Mum
M.B.

Reading Consultant: Prue Goodwin, Lecturer in literacy and children's books

ORCHARD BOOKS
338 Euston Road, London NW1 3BH
Orchard Books Australia
Level 17/207 Kent Street, Sydney, NSW 2000

First published in 2012
First paperback publication in 2013

ISBN 978 1 40831 212 4 (hardback)
ISBN 978 1 40831 220 9 (paperback)

A CIP catalogue record for this book is available
from the British Library.

1 3 5 7 9 10 8 6 4 2 (hardback)
1 3 5 7 9 10 8 6 4 2 (paperback)

Printed in Great Britain

Orchard Books is a division of Hachette Children's Books,
an Hachette UK company.

www.hachette.co.uk

Fairy Tale
Twists

The Not-So-Evil
Stepmother

Written by Katie Dale
Illustrated by Matt Buckingham

ORCHARD

"Once upon a time," I read,
"a prince and pretty maiden wed,
and both lived happily ever after..."
But listen, folks – there's nothing dafter!

Don't fall for it — don't be deceived,
they sucked me in, I too believed.
The tales said once I was a bride
then I'd be happy — but they LIED!

I found myself a lovely bloke,
strong and kind (though stony broke).

He had two kids, so cute and sweet –
"At last!" I thought. "My life's complete!"
But not long after we were wed…

My darling husband dropped down dead!

I tried to be a good stepmother
to young Gretel and her brother.
But, alas, I'm sad to say,
the naughty children ran away!

I searched for days throughout the wood,
but sadly they were lost for good.

Then, one day, in the dead of night,
I woke to get a dreadful fright...

A man was standing by my bed!
"Marry me, my love!" he said.
The man was tall, and handsome, too.
All my insides turned to goo.

I stared at him, and then we kissed.
(I was quite helpless to resist.)
Then lightning! Fireworks! Saints above!
It was a kiss of Truest Love!

So this was where I'd gone awry!
I hadn't married the right guy!
"Be mine!" my love begged. I agreed.
Well, if at first you don't succeed...

He took me home, and golly, gosh!
He clearly wasn't short of dosh!
The house was huge, it towered high,
its turrets nearly touched the sky.

The windowsills were made of pearl.
"Gee-whiz, are you some kind of earl?"
He laughed. "No, just a Count," he said.
"You'll be a Countess when we're wed."

"A Countess? Me? No way, you're kidding!"
"You'll have maids to do your bidding,
butlers too, and cooks of course,
and darling, would you like a horse?"

(I tell you, folks, right there and then
I *believed* the tales again –
I really thought that this could be
my happy ending – silly me.)

He smiled, "Now come with me, my sweet,
there's someone I'd like you to meet –
my only daughter, darling Snow."

Another *stepdaughter*? Oh NO!

"Pleased to meet you, I'm Snow White."

She had her father's looks all right.
I've never seen a girl so fair –
such milky skin and jet-black hair!

I felt quite frumpy by her side.
"But dear, you'll make a gorgeous bride –
just look," Count smiled. "What do you see?"
I shrugged. "It's only plain old me."

He shook his head, turned to the wall.
"Who is the fairest of them all?"
"Why, Count," the looking-glass replied.
"No question, it's your future bride!"

My jaw fell open. "Holy cow!
That mirror *spoke* to you – but how?"

"It's magic – all it
says is true.
It's my engagement
gift to you."

A magic mirror? Holy crow!

"Look – your reflection doesn't show!"

"I fade beside someone so fair,"
he smiled. "You are beyond compare."
Was he the perfect guy, or what?
Charming, loving, rich – and hot!

The days dragged till my wedding-date.
When it arrived, I couldn't wait!

I rushed inside to find my groom.
"My love!" I called through every room…

I searched for him upstairs and down,
(not easy in a wedding-gown!)…

…till finally I found a door
I hadn't come across before.
I pushed it open and I found…

…a coffin lying on the ground.

He looked so handsome, even dead,
as if he was asleep in bed…
I took Snow White and left that day.
I packed our things, moved far away.

I hid my tears and broken heart,
and tried to make a fresh new start.
But poor Snow White seemed really sad.
"Of course," I thought. "She needs a dad."

So husband number three was Pete –
not much to look at, but quite sweet.
He did his best for me and Snow,
he grew us veggies, row on row.

But then, right on our wedding day,
we found Snow White had run away!
"Oh no!" I cried. "Oh, not again!"
I searched the countryside in vain.

Till finally, upon the grass,
I found a coffin made of glass.
"It cannot be!" I wailed. "Oh no!
First my Count, now darling Snow!"

Just like her dad, Snow seemed to sleep,
while seven dwarves began to weep.

"She ate this apple – just one bite –
then dropped down dead! Oh, poor Snow White!"

So, sadly, I returned alone,
and had some children of my own.

A son came first, and then twin daughters:

Peter struggled to support us…
till one day his heart gave out
while digging up a stubborn sprout.

The fridge grew bare — the kids just grew.
All our bills were overdue.
I *had* to raise some cash — but how?
I sent Jack off to sell the cow.

Instead, the boy returned with beans!
(He'd got his father's love of greens.)

I got so mad I threw them out,
but then the beans began to sprout...
They grew and grew, so tall and high,
above the clouds and through the sky.
Before I caught him, up climbed Jack –
"Wait!" I shouted. "Son – come back!"

So that left me, Rose Red and Bella.

Then came Reg and Cinderella.

Reg was old, but he was funny.

More than that – the bloke had money.

But, just after we were wed,
yes – you've guessed it – Reg dropped dead.
I did my best to raise his child,
but she was spoilt and rude and wild.

She teased my girls and pulled their hair,

she hogged their things, and wouldn't share.

I bit my tongue, though it was tough.
She'd lost her dad – it must be rough.

I organised for us to all
go, as a family, to the ball.
I hoped that it would break the ice.
We each dressed up, all posh and nice…

But then Rose Red ran through the hall.
She hollered, "Stuff the stupid ball!
I'm off to visit Gran instead!"
She slammed the door and then she fled.

I rushed upstairs. "What happened, girls?"
My Belle was combing Cinders' curls.

I said, "Hang on, that's Rose Red's dress!"
Young Cinderella smiled, "Well, yes.
She gave it to me – *GENTLE*, Belle! –
she loaned me these fab rings as well."
Cinders beamed. "Rose Red's so sweet!
Now Bella dear, massage my feet!"

"Do no such thing!" I ordered Bella.
"What's the deal here, Cinderella?"
She rolled her eyes. "Oh honey, *chill*!
I just showed Rose Red Daddy's will…"

He'd left young Cinders every penny!
My twins and I weren't getting any!
She laughed. "Do everything I say,
or I could kick you out today!"

"That's it!" I cried. "Enough!
You're grounded!"
Cinders looked at me, astounded.
"*You* can't ground me!" she replied,
and so I locked her up inside.

Despite her tricks, the ball went well.
Prince Charming even married Belle!
And Rose Red found herself a man
while visiting her poorly Gran.

And Cind's now happy as can be –
she too wed into royalty.
They married just the other day –
I even caught her big bouquet…

I'm thrilled they've all found wedded bliss,
but yes, of course, I'll always miss
my kids and stepkids – every one.
The house feels empty now they've gone.

I sighed, "There's no point in pretending –
I'll never get a happy ending."
"Don't be daft!" a voice replied.
I jumped up. "Who said that?" I cried.

"The magic mirror! Oh, hello!
I thought I'd lost you years ago!"

"Oh, no more husbands, please!" I said.
"They broke my heart when they all died.
I'm cursed to live alone," I sighed.

"Not this time – the time is right –
you'll find your happy end tonight."

"Tonight?" I scoffed. "Uh-huh. Yeah, sure."
Just then a knock came at the door.
I stared at it. "Who could that be?"

"Well, don't just stand there – go and see!"

My heart beat fast. "It can't be true!"

"My love!" Count cried. "It's really you!

I've searched for you throughout the land!"

"But darling – I don't understand –

I thought you'd died!"

He shook his head.

"I have a secret, love," he said.

He whispered softly in my ear,
then asked, "Can you still love me, dear?"
"You mean you'll have eternal life?
Yippee! Of *course* I'll be your wife!"
So I wed my True Love at last.
We kissed and boogied, had a blast…

But best of all, my kids came back –
Hansel, Gretel, Belle and Jack,
Rose Red, Snow White and all their friends,
and even Cinders made amends.

"Who said happy ends were daft...?"
The mirror smiled, but I just laughed.
We all lived happily together,
forever – and ever – and ever – and EVER!

Fairy Tale Twists

Written by Katie Dale
Illustrated by Matt Buckingham

All priced at £4.99

Orchard Books are available from all good bookshops,
or can be ordered from our website, www.orchardbooks.co.uk,
or telephone 01235 827702, or fax 01235 827703.